# Jet the Cat...

For Mabel, a kid unlike any other kid — P. C.

For Tucker & Rylee, my kitty best friends — T. R.

Barefoot Books
Bradford Mill, 23 Bradford Street
West Concord, MA 01742

Barefoot Books
29/30 Fitzroy Square
London, W1T 6LQ

Text copyright © 2021 by Phaea Crede
Illustrations copyright © 2021 by Terry Runyan
The moral rights of Phaea Crede and Terry Runyan have been asserted

First published in United States of America by Barefoot Books, Inc
and in Great Britain by Barefoot Books, Ltd in 2021

Graphic design by Sarah Soldano, Barefoot Books
Edited and art directed by Lisa Rosinsky, Barefoot Books
Reproduction by Bright Arts, Hong Kong
Printed in China on 100% acid-free paper
This book was typeset in A Font with Serifs,
Amalfi, DJB Dear St. Nick, Fiddleshticks,
Hoagie, Sassoon Infant and SugarSweet
The artwork was created with digital techniques

Hardcover ISBN 978-1-64686-166-8
Paperback ISBN 978-1-64686-167-5
E-book ISBN 978-1-64686-259-7

British Cataloguing-in-Publication Data: a catalogue record
for this book is available from the British Library

Library of Congress Cataloging-in-Publication Data
is available under LCCN 2020949644

1 3 5 7 9 8 6 4 2

# ...Is NOT a Cat?!

written by Phaea Crede

illustrated by Terry Runyan

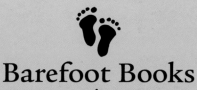

**Barefoot Books**
Step inside a story

Jet is a **CAT** just like any other **CAT**.
She loves to pounce. She loves to sprawl.
And, of course, she loves to swim.
She loves to swim all day
until the sun goes down.
And even a little bit after.

Just like any other cat!

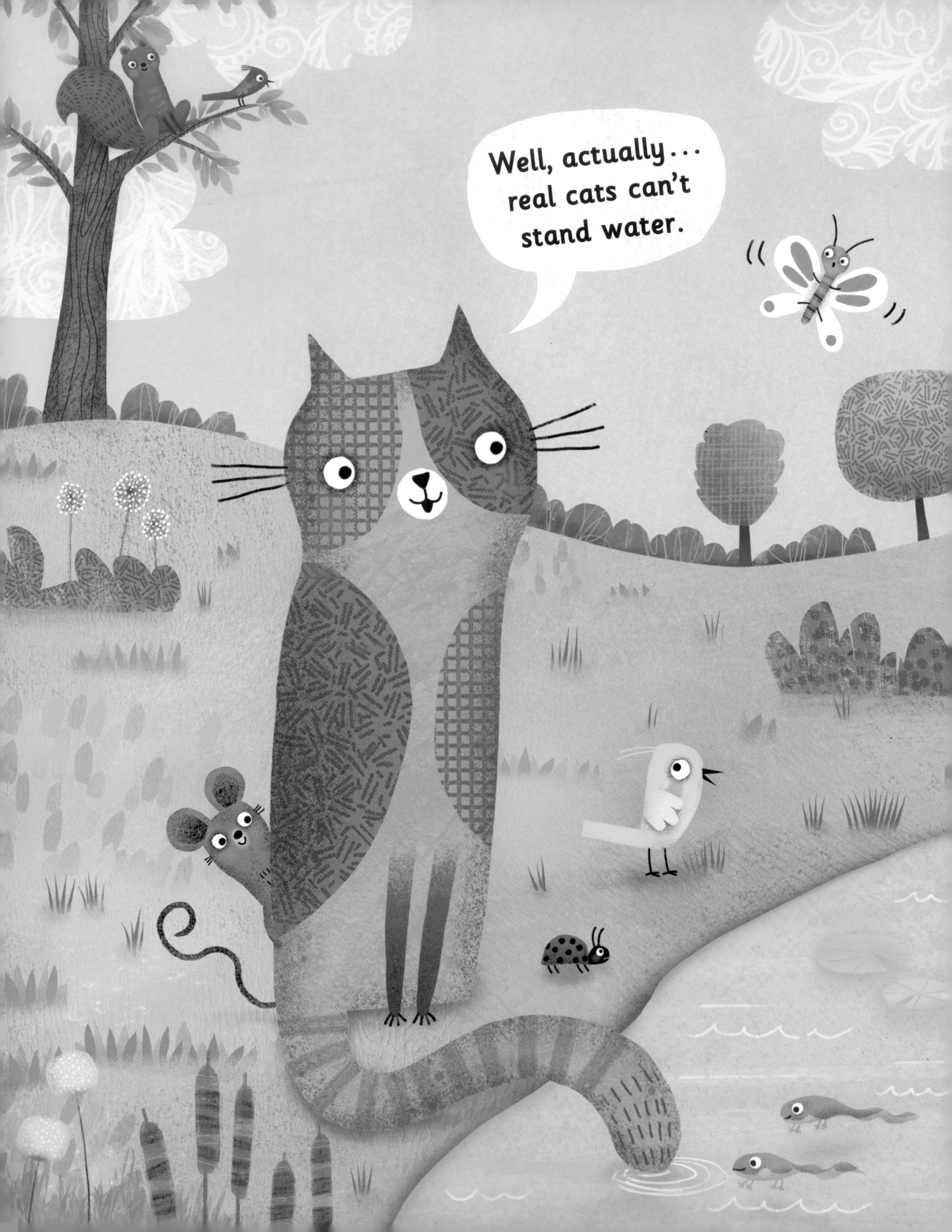
Well, actually . . . real cats can't stand water.

"We can't?" asks Jet.
"WE can't," says Tom the Cat.
"YOU are not a CAT. You are a FROG."
"Huh," says Jet. And with a shrug,
she dives back in.

Jet is a FROG just like any other FROG.
She loves to swim. She loves to eat bugs.
And, of course, she sings in a high voice.

Meeeooooww!

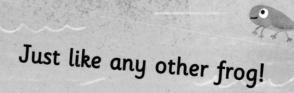

Just like any other frog!

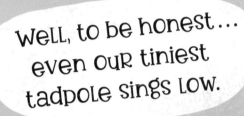

"Really truly?" asks Jet.

"Truly really," says Bull the Frog.

"YOU are not a FROG. You are a BIRD."

"Weird," says Jet.

And with a sigh, she climbs on up.

Jet is a **BIRD** just like any other **BIRD**.
She loves to eat bugs. She loves to sing high.
And, of course, when she jumps from a tree
she falls flat.

Just like any other bird!

"That's not true," says Jet.
"Oh, it's true," says Blue the Bird.
"YOU are not a BIRD. You are a GOAT!"

"Harrumph," says Jet.
And with a grunt, she trots off.

Jet is a **GOAT** just like any other **GOAT**.
Totally flightless? Check. Born to prance? You know it!
And, of course, she's completely beard-free.

Just like any other goat!

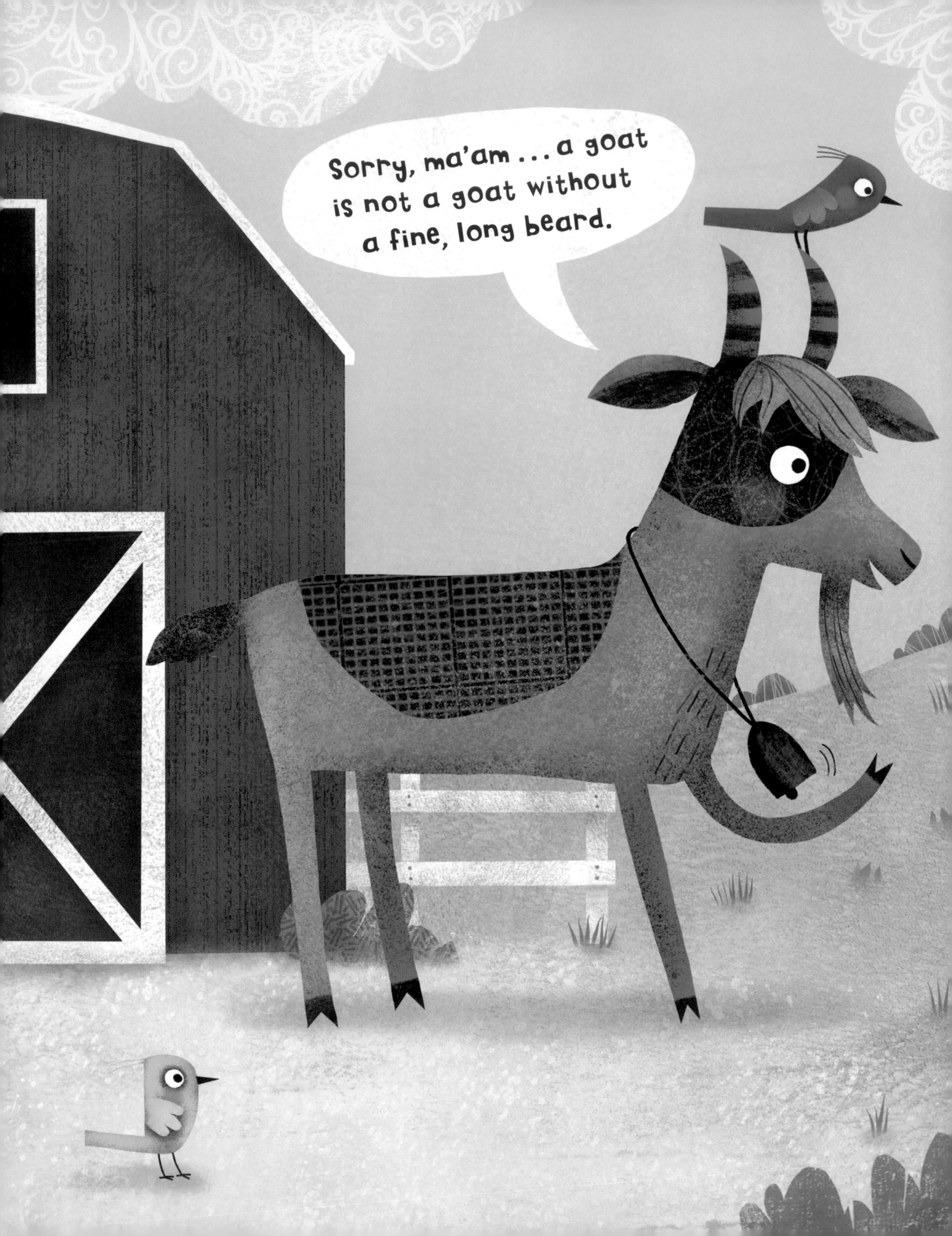
Sorry, ma'am . . . a goat is not a goat without a fine, long beard.

"No way," says Jet.
"Oh, way," says Bill the Goat.
"YOU are not a **GOAT**. You are a . . ."

...pig!
No... maybe a mole? A skunk? A skink?
Platypus? Sun bear? Goblin shark?
Pink fairy armadillo?
Friendly school librarian?

"I can't do this anymore!" wails Jet.

Jet goes home for a nice, long swim.
She feels like herself again.
Now she has something to say to all those creatures
still arguing about what she can or cannot be.

"Listen up!" says Jet.

"I am a **CAT** UNLIKE any other CAT.
But I'm still a CAT. And a great **CAT** at that.
Now if you'll excuse me, I have to work on my backstroke."

But as she turns to go...

"Well," grins **Jet the Cat**, "what's wrong with that?"

Then they all swim, run,
sing, explore and play around
until the sun goes down.

And even a little bit after.